THE GIFT

A NOVEL BY

FREIDA MCFADDEN

The Gift

To my darling husband

NOVELS BY FREIDA McFADDEN

Never Lie

The Inmate

The Housemaid

Do You Remember?

Do Not Disturb

The Locked Door

Want to Know a Secret?

One by One

The Wife Upstairs

The Perfect Son

The Ex

The Surrogate Mother

Brain Damage

Baby City

Suicide Med

The Devil Wears Scrubs

The Devil You Know

CHAPTER 1

There's nothing worse than being dirt poor on Christmas.

Actually, I take that back. Working a double shift on Christmas Eve at a diner in the Bronx is pretty bad too. But if I don't do it, I won't be able to scrape together enough money to pay the rent this month. And if there's one thing decidedly worse than being dirt poor on Christmas, it's being dirt poor *and* homeless on Christmas.

Working the double shift today might not be as bad if it were at some respectable diner, where people came in with their families on Christmas Eve and left nice, hefty tips that I could use to supplement my insultingly, crushingly low salary. But no. I work at Stevie's, which I'm convinced must have a sign on the door saying, "Come in to order coffee and nothing else." At any given time, I am pouring refills for half of my customers, who then tip in coins only, many of them copper.

Have you ever picked pennies out of a mostly empty coffee cup? I have. Every day.

The only good thing I can say is that the shift is almost

over. Stevie's is closing for the night at eleven p.m., three hours earlier than its usual closing time, and then I get to go home to my husband, Justin, to enjoy what we have left of Christmas Eve.

"I can't wait to get out of here," my coworker Bessie tells me. She is sitting at one of the empty tables, organizing a pile of clean silverware, and I am sitting at a table a few feet away, waiting for the last few stragglers to finish up their damn coffee. "The second I get home, I am going to get right in the bathtub and soak till the sun comes up."

I grunt in agreement. I've been on my feet for the last twelve hours. Even my blisters have blisters. That's not an exaggeration—I found a blister the other day that had another blister growing from it. They should write me up in a medical journal.

Bessie raises her eyebrows at me. "How about you, Stella? You got plans with Justin?" She lets out a raspy cough, which she has had since I've been working here for the last two years, and seems to get worse every day. "Maybe a bath *with* him."

"I'll just be happy if we have hot water," I say. We were late paying our heating bill, so we had to do without heat for a little while. It's supposed to be back on today though—a nice little Christmas present.

"Well," she says, "you got your honey to keep you warm."

Justin and I have spent a lot of time cuddling on the sofa to take advantage of body heat since the actual heat got shut off. He's also been spending more time at the law school library. He is in his second year, which is why I am mostly paying the bills. Waitressing is my second job, the first being a preschool job that allows me to utilize my early childhood education degree, all at minimum wage. Four years of college, tons of debt, and I need two jobs just to pay the bills. I should have majored in Not Being Poor.

Bessie lets out a yawn, rubbing her eyes, which smears her heavy mascara. She's twice my age, and she wears twice as much makeup. "What do you think it would take to get everybody to leave right this minute?" she whispers to me. "I mean, what kind of psychopath wants coffee at a quarter to eleven?"

I let my gaze sweep over the dreary diner. Even though Bessie and I have scrubbed down all the tables, they all have a layer of thick grime that we can't get off. Even in broad daylight, Stevie's never looks bright or cheery—but at night, it sometimes feels like being in a morgue. The overhead lights keep flickering, but the two remaining patrons don't seem to notice. One is a man who hasn't taken his coat or hat off the entire time he's been here sipping coffee, and the other is an elderly woman all the way in a booth in the back.

Fifteen more minutes. Fifteen minutes, then we can officially throw these two people out on the street, and I can go home.

I grab a hair elastic out of my purse and gather my blond hair back into a bun behind my head. Most of the waitresses wear their hair up for their shift, but I have found that my tips are at least twice as high when I keep my hair down. (Of course, twice practically nothing is still practically nothing.) My hair is the color of corn silk and is my best feature by far—people constantly compliment me on my hair and occasionally reach out to try to touch it. I haven't done more than trim it in the last decade, so it runs all the way down my back, silky and shiny.

I skimp on everything else. I hardly sleep. I skip meals. I'm wearing the same winter coat I've had for the last five years. But I *always* take care of my hair. I have very ordinary features, and without my hair, I would be very plain. When people call me pretty, that's why. It's certainly not because of my thin lips or eyes that are too close together.

After my hair is out of my face, I pull out my phone to distract myself. I scan through the news reports for interesting stories. This guy won the Powerball lottery last week with a huge jackpot, and now there's a new story about that same guy—apparently, he dropped dead of a heart attack the very next day. Crazy.

I don't see any messages from Justin, so I send him one of my own:

I can't wait to celebrate our first married Christmas together.

Three dots appear on the screen, and after a minute, his reply appears:

Can't wait either. When are you getting home?

Justin and I got married over the summer, after being together for the last two years. It was a beautiful ceremony, even if it did rain that day. This is our first Christmas as husband and wife, which makes it special. He's been very stressed lately with school, and things have been a bit tense between us, so that makes me even more determined for us to have a great holiday together. I tap out a quick reply:

I'll be leaving at 11.

His response appears almost instantly:

I'll be waiting. I think we should exchange gifts at midnight.

My stomach sinks. I've always been really into Christmas presents, but this year, I've come up short. When you can't even pay your heating bill, you're not getting anyone a nice present. It's just not happening. For example, I got my mother a hat and matching gloves from the dollar store. I got my father an iPhone charger, also from the dollar store. The dollar store was my best friend during this holiday season.

But I couldn't bring myself to get Justin a present at the dollar store. He means more to me than that, and I want him to know it. A candle that smells like apple cider just doesn't say I love you.

Except how do you get the perfect present for the man you love when you have no money?

"What's wrong, Stella?" Bessie asks. "You got a troubled look on your face."

I grimace. "I never got Justin a Christmas present. And he wants to exchange presents tonight. Even if I could afford to get him anything, all the stores are closed."

"Well, maybe something from the diner…" Bessie snatches up a piece of silverware from one of the piles she's made. "Here ya go. Nothing says I love you like a fork."

"Bessie…"

She picks a napkin up from another pile on the table. "I bet you could turn this into some sort of origami crane."

Great. I should have gotten him a gift from the dollar store while I still could. "I wanted to give him something really special this year," I tell her. "I mean, it's our first Christmas as husband and wife."

Bessie looks unimpressed. She has been married three times, so she doesn't get it. "It's just a present. I bet he's not putting as much thought into it as you are."

I'm not so sure about that. Even though Justin and I agreed not to spend too much on presents for each other, he has made a big deal over this being our first married Christmas. He's probably got some incredibly thoughtful gift, and I'm going to look like a heartless grinch when I show up with nothing.

The guy with the eternal hat and coat finally shuffles out of his seat. He tosses two dollars on the table, which barely covers the cost of his coffee, then he pushes past us without saying a word. The bell on the door jingles as he leaves, taking with him the vague odor of urine.

"Merry Christmas!" Bessie calls out, even though he's already gone.

I check my watch—two minutes left until eleven o'clock. The old lady in the corner is still sitting there, and she's making no move to leave. I'm not sure if she realizes that we're closing, and I need to tell her. I have a bad feeling she is going to be one of the many customers who suddenly realizes she has misplaced her wallet. If she has, I guess we'll just let her leave. It's not like we're going to call the police on Christmas Eve to report a little old lady who can't pay for her turkey club and fries.

"I'm going to tell the old lady we're closing soon," I say

to Bessie. "Does she have her check?"

Bessie raises a shoulder. "How should I know? You're the one who waited on her."

"No, I didn't. That was your table."

"Nuh-uh. Corner table was yours."

"*No.*" I grit my teeth. "I think I would know if I waited on her."

"And I wouldn't?"

I glance over at the old woman, sitting at that booth all alone. "So are you saying nobody waited on that woman the whole time she's been here?"

"Since it's just the two of us here, I'm thinking no."

I frown. "How long has she been sitting there?"

Bessie looks down at her fingernails, which are sharp enough to maul someone if she needs to. She says they're useful protection during her walk home. "At least an hour. Maybe more. Every time I've looked, she's been sitting there."

I pat the bun on the back of my head. "Let me go talk to her."

My chair scrapes against the linoleum floor as I get to my feet. My blisters—adult and baby—scream in pain, but I comfort myself with the knowledge that I will soon be home with my wonderful husband. And no, I don't have a present for him, but I will find a way to make it up to him. If I can ever get out of this place.

My footsteps echo through the diner as I make my way down the aisle to the booth at the very end, where the old woman is sitting. The cheap leather on the booth has ripped in several places, exposing yellow foam. Sure enough, the woman doesn't have any food in front of her. She's got a napkin with a fork and knife, but nobody has even served her a glass of water.

I don't understand. If she's been sitting here for over an hour, why didn't she try to get our attention to wait on her?

As I get closer, I can make out the wrinkled features on her face. She has a broad nose, and her lips seem to be swallowed up by her gaping mouth. Her gray hair is twisted into a bun as thick as mine.

But the most noticeable thing about her is her eyes. They look like they were once a penetrating black color, but they've grown cloudy from cataracts. And as I walk toward her, they don't blink. They stare forward as she sits in the booth, slightly slumped, unnaturally still.

"Ma'am?" I say.

She doesn't move. She doesn't turn in my direction or say a word.

"Ma'am," I try again. "We… uh, we're closing soon."

Once again, it's like she's not even aware that anyone is around her. Her body is completely rigid.

Oh my God.

I think she's dead.

CHAPTER 2

"Bessie!" I scream. "*Bessie!*"

Oh my God, this is the worst Christmas Eve ever. Not only have I been working two shifts in a row at a crappy diner, but after forgetting to serve one of my customers, she *died*. You would think that if you screw up as a waitress, the worst thing that could happen is somebody has a bad meal. But apparently not. Apparently, my neglect has *killed* this woman. She *starved* to death while waiting for one of us to bring her food.

I am worse than Scrooge. I definitely deserve coal in my stocking. (Instead of a bunch of stuff from the dollar store, which is probably what is actually in my stocking.)

Bessie comes hurrying over, looking about as panicked as I feel. She catches sight of the old woman and sucks in a breath. "Is she…?"

"I think she's gone," I squeak.

This is going to be so awful. We will have to call the police, and then… Well, I'm not sure what will happen next. I imagine her family will be notified. Her children and grandchildren will find out that their mother/grandmother won't be around to open presents with them on Christmas morning. Way to ruin the holidays.

Or what if she doesn't have a family? After all, she is all alone on Christmas Eve. What if nobody even cares that she died? That's even more horrible.

"What do we do?" I whisper to Bessie, as if the woman might overhear us if I'm too loud.

"Lady!" Bessie snaps, getting right up in her face. "We're closing! Time to wake up!"

Still nothing. Oh God, she's definitely dead. How long has a dead woman been sitting here with us?

"Let me take a look at her purse," Bessie says. "Maybe she's got identification."

"Shouldn't we call the police?"

"Yeah, but first, let's check her purse."

I get the distinct feeling that Bessie doesn't care about identification, and she's just hoping to score a few bucks off the dead woman before the police haul her away to the morgue. I can't even contemplate doing something like that. Yes, I like to have electricity and heat in our apartment, but I'm not stealing from a dead woman. You have to draw the line somewhere, and that's mine.

But as Bessie reaches for the woman's alligator skin purse, a wrinkled hand shoots out and grabs her forearm.

Bessie lets out an ear-shattering scream as she backs away from the old lady, who apparently is very much alive.

"I'm so sorry!" I cry. "We thought… I mean, we were worried that you were…"

The old woman finally blinks at me. She might be alive, but I very well could have a heart attack right about now. Bessie doesn't look much better. The woman wipes a fleck of drool from the corner of her mouth and stares up at us.

"Yes?" she says in an accent that sounds European.

I wring my hands together. "We… we're closing." I glance down at my watch. "Like, now."

The old woman considers this for a moment. Finally, she nods and carefully extracts herself from the booth. We don't have a check for her to pay, but it doesn't seem like she ate anything, so I guess it's okay. I almost offer her a cup of coffee, considering we screwed up and failed to wait on her, but the thought of staying here even another minute is too horrible to bear.

The woman slowly pulls on an extremely worn wool coat, then limps in the direction of the exit. She looks like she's about to fall over and probably should have a cane or a walker, but I'm not in any position to judge.

"Merry Christmas!" I call out as cheerfully as I can muster. And I do feel a little cheerful. After all, I'm going home soon to my wonderful and handsome husband.

Although most of all, I am tired. Bone tired. I'll be lucky if I can keep my eyes open while Justin and I are exchanging gifts. Not that I have a gift to exchange with him.

The old woman turns to look at me. She stops walking and reaches for her purse.

Oh God, what now? Is she going to take a gun out and rob us? Is that the punchline to this evening?

"I hear your problem," the old woman says in her slightly broken English. "I want to help you."

My problem? My problem is that it is Christmas Eve, I'm tired, and I want to go home. But I stand there patiently while the woman rifles around in her purse until she pulls out what looks like a business card. She holds it out to me.

"Take," she says.

Obligingly, I take the card out of her hand. It is, in fact, a business card. Emblazoned in block letters on the card are the words: HELGA'S ATTIC. Followed by an address about a dozen blocks away from here.

"What is this?" I ask.

"This is my store," the old woman says. "I am Helga."

"Oh," I say.

"I will help you find a Christmas present for your husband."

"Oh." I force an apologetic smile. "Actually, I don't have any money for that."

"Not a problem. We will make a deal."

Bessie has been listening to this exchange, and she suddenly speaks up, "So it's a pawn shop?"

The woman, Helga, nods thoughtfully. "I am always willing to purchase interesting items."

I almost tell her I don't have anything worth buying, but then I remember I am wearing a necklace that my aunt and uncle gave me as a graduation gift. Maybe that's worth something. And anyway, anything I could find at this shop is better than coming home empty-handed. Plus, it's on the way.

"It's late though," I point out. "You're still going to be open?"

"I am *always* open," Helga says. "It is important to have a present for your husband for the holidays. I always have presents for my Sven and my daughter."

I look down at my watch. I really just want to go home, but at the same time, I'm desperate to find a present for Justin. It is our first Christmas together as a married couple, and I want to get him something *amazing*.

"You come," Helga says. It's not a question—it's a command. "I will find you the perfect gift."

With those words, Helga turns and leaves the diner. The bells on the door jingle when she leaves—for just a bit longer than they should.

As soon as she is gone, Bessie turns to me and clutches her chest. "Oh my God, that woman scared me half to death. I thought she was rising from the dead!"

"Yeah," I agree. My heart is still racing a bit.

"You're not going to go to that crazy store of hers, are you?"

"Maybe," I admit. "It's on the way home, and I really do want to get something special for Justin."

"Why bother?" Bessie again grabs a utensil from the table and holds it out to me. "I'm telling you, every guy just wants a nice fork."

"Okay, okay. I get it."

"Anyway, you should get out of here. Go home to your husband. I'll finish cleaning and lock up."

"You sure?"

"Yeah, I don't have anyone to go home to. Get out of here, and don't bother with that stupid store."

Maybe because she's been married three times, Bessie doesn't have a sense of romance like I do. I can't go home without a Christmas present for my husband. I *can't*.

I'll stop by Helga's store to find something nice and reasonably priced. And if there's nothing good, I simply won't buy anything. It's on the way home, so I have nothing to lose.

What's the worst that could happen?

CHAPTER 3

As I'm walking to Helga's store, it starts to snow.

I've always thought that Christmas snow is good luck. So my mood lifts considerably as the tiny white snowflakes land on the shoulders of my coat and my sky-blue beanie. This is an omen—I'm sure of it.

Helga's Attic is about ten blocks away from the diner. It's a small, nondescript store that I might have walked past a dozen times in the last couple of years. The inside is dark, and for a moment, I'm certain I misunderstood that old woman, and she meant I should come back after the holidays, but then a light goes on inside the store. I try the door, and it opens.

This store is like nothing I have ever seen before. It almost looks like an antique store, but it's full of smaller items, ranging from the commonplace to the bizarre. Helga is nowhere to be seen, so I take a moment to browse. The shelf right in front of me contains a picture frame, a ceramic vase that has foreign-looking markings on it, and a skull.

My gaze lingers on the skull. Based on the size, it looks

to be a human skull. Is it a replica? A remnant dug up from an ancient burial site? What is this woman doing with a *human skull*?

Maybe I don't want to know.

A loud sound from the back startles me, and I jump away from the skull. A second later, Helga shuffles out, wearing a billowy dress. As soon as she sees me, she smiles, her lips completely vanishing into the hole of her mouth.

"Stella, is it?" she says.

Did I tell her my name? I don't remember telling her, but she must have overheard Bessie saying it. "Yes."

She places her fingertips together. "So you wish to purchase a Christmas present for your husband?"

I nod eagerly. "You said you might accept a trade, and I have a necklace that I think is worth a good amount."

"Very good, then. Let me show you some items he might enjoy."

The temperature is below freezing outside, but it's very warm in Helga's store. So warm that when she leads me deeper into the store, sweat breaks out on the back of my neck. I pull off my hat and stuff it into my pocket. I don't know why it's so hot in here, especially with the large windows. It's almost as if the items in the store are radiating heat.

"This is a very interesting gift." Helga plucks something off a shelf that almost looks like a hand, but it's covered in fur. "Sven acquired it during a trip to India."

"What is it?"

"It is a monkey's paw," she says. "The man who sold it to my husband told him that the paw would grant three wishes to the owner."

I roll my eyes. "Oh *really*?"

"This could be… quite lucrative."

"Or how about I trade my necklace for some magic beans?"

Helga's lips twitch. "Very well. Let us keep looking then."

The next item she pulls off the shelf is a doll. This antique item is about two feet tall, wearing a pink dress with lace trim, with a bow tie around her waist. Her frozen plastic face smiles up at me. "What about this Talking Tina doll? It belonged to my daughter."

Before I can protest, she pulls a string in the back. A child-like voice says, "My name is Talking Tina, and I love you very much!"

I stare at Helga. "I told you that my husband is a grown man, right? Why on earth would he want a *talking doll*?"

She shrugs. "I do not understand what young people like. For a little while, every man who came to my store only wanted to buy toy ponies. Rainbow Dash this, Pinkie Pie that. I do not judge. If you are a grown man and want a pony, I will sell you a pony."

"My husband does not want a toy pony, and he does not want a doll." I press my lips together. "I would really like to get home. If you don't have anything—"

"Wait."

I follow Helga's path as she shuffles across the shop to a small desk at the other end. When she's behind the desk, she rummages around in one of the drawers. Finally, she pulls out a gleaming silver chain.

"This is a very nice item," she says.

It is indeed exquisite. The shine of it catches the light overhead, no matter which way you turn it. "What is it, exactly?"

"It is a pocket watch chain."

My breath catches in my throat. One of Justin's prized possessions is a pocket watch that his father gave him before he died. Like the chain, it is sterling silver, and Justin always brags that it keeps perfect time and will probably be around long after he and I are gone.

He loves that pocket watch. I'm not saying that he loves the watch more than he loves me, but if there were a fire, and he could only save me or the watch... well, hopefully, it won't come down to that.

In any case, this gift is absolutely perfect. Way better than anything I could have gotten at the dollar store. I can tell by how heavy it is that it's expensive, and Justin will realize how much I love him when I give it to him at midnight.

"I love it," I say. "It's perfect."

Her lips quirk up. She has smiled at me a few times, but I have never seen any teeth in her mouth. I'm wondering if she has any. "I thought it might be."

I reach inside my T-shirt and dig out the necklace with the heart pendant on it. It was a gift from my aunt and uncle, but I don't have much of an attachment to it. I'm happy to part with it to get this chain for Justin.

I lay the necklace on the desk in front of Helga. She picks it up, her cloudy eyes inspecting the links—God knows how she can see anything with those obscured pupils, though. She takes her time, examining it with surprisingly steady hands. Finally, she lays it back down on the table.

"How much for the necklace?" I ask.

"One dollar," she says.

My mouth drops open. "One dollar? Are you serious? That was a graduation gift."

"Cheap graduation gift," she sneers. "Cheap material, all the gems fake. Worth nothing. Not even a dollar."

Great. Thanks for nothing, Aunt Jean and Uncle Howard.

"I don't think I have anything else," I say helplessly. "How much is the watch chain, anyway?"

Helga taps on a little white tag I hadn't noticed that is

stuck to the chain. I turn it over to look at the price, and my heart sinks. Oh well. I guess Justin isn't getting a watch chain for Christmas.

"Sorry," I mumble. "There's no way I can afford that."

The elderly woman shakes her head. "I told you. We can make a trade."

"I have nothing else to trade."

"You have one thing." A smile creeps across her lips. "You have very beautiful hair, my dear."

Instinctively, I reach for my silky blond locks, still pinned behind my head. "Thank you."

"Did I tell you I also make and sell wigs in this store?"

Helga points to the corner of the store, and sure enough, there is an assortment of exquisitely beautiful wigs, mounted on plastic heads. I've worn wigs a couple of times to costume parties, but nothing like that. These look incredibly realistic.

"Very nice," I say. "But what does that—"

Oh. *Oh*. Oh my God.

"No." I back away from the desk. "I'm sorry, but *no*. No way. That's… out of the question."

"Is it though?"

"*Yes*."

"Think about it, Stella." Helga comes around the side of the desk. "Hair grows back. Hair is fleeting. But your husband—he will remember this Christmas for the rest of your lives. Your first Christmas together. And you come home with *nothing*?" Her lips curl in disgust. "How can you build a life together based on that? He will always resent you."

"I'll get him something else then," I say desperately. "What about that picture frame? Or the creepy monkey hand thingy?"

"You can afford nothing in this store," she hisses at me. "The only way you will leave here with a gift for your husband who you love so much is to make this trade."

My knees buckle. Every bone in my body is screaming out that this is the wrong thing to do. And yet…

I can't come home tonight with nothing. She's right— he will never forget it. And knowing Justin, I'm certain he has something amazing for me.

And hair *does* grow back, right?

CHAPTER 4

Helga leads me to a back room behind the store that is illuminated by a single bulb hanging from the ceiling. The room is basically a storage room, filled with items that are clearly rejects from the rest of the store. There's a large amount of clothing, piled into cardboard boxes, several lamps with crooked shades, and a mannequin wearing one dress on top of another and a purple wig. The mannequin is very much creeping me out.

Helga closes the door behind us. Then she locks it. A tiny part of me is scared that Helga's game the whole time was to trap me in this room and keep me here as her hostage—possibly to teach me a lesson for forgetting to wait on her tonight. Then again, it's not like nobody knows I'm here—I told Bessie I would stop by. Also, I think I could take Helga in a fight.

So I'm not *too* worried. But I am a *little* worried.

"Sit," Helga instructs me.

She points with her gnarled hand at a wooden chair in

the center of the room. There's a small table set up next to the chair, and on top of it is a pair of kitchen scissors, several hair ties, and an electric razor.

I hesitate, looking at the array of equipment that Helga has assembled. Do I really want this watch chain that badly? Maybe this is all a mistake.

"Sit!" Helga barks at me.

"Listen," I say, "I'm not sure if I want to do this…"

The old woman stares up at me with her cloudy lenses. "It is up to you. Someday you will think back on this Christmas and how your vanity got in the way of buying a meaningful present for your husband."

I take a deep breath. She's right. Justin would love that watch chain, and the fact that I have to sacrifice something so meaningful to get it for him makes it even more special.

This will be the best Christmas we will ever have.

I settle down on the hard wooden chair and remove my coat. Before I even have a chance to hang the coat on the back of the chair, Helga is getting to work undoing my bun. Despite her arthritic-looking hands, she is quickly able to smooth out my hair and gets to work tying the thick blond strands into six separate braids.

I'm doing this for you, Justin. Because I love you so much.

The braids run up to the root of my hair, close to my skull. "Do you have to braid them all the way to my scalp? I don't know if I want my hair to be that short."

"Yes," Helga says in a clipped tone. "This is how it must be done."

I can still stop her. She has not used her scissors yet. But it feels like I have reached the point of no return. I am doing this. And I don't *want* to stop her. I want to give Justin this gift. I want to make this sacrifice for him.

Helga reaches for the scissors. The first snip tugs on my scalp, and it feels so strange after the hair comes free. With five more snips, my head feels much lighter. Like I might float away.

This is actually quite nice. I love my hair, but it feels good to be free of it. And think of all the money I will save on shampoo!

The buzz of the electric razor interrupts my thoughts. I jerk my head away. "What are you doing?"

"I must even it out," Helga tells me like I'm stupid for asking. "Now you look like a crazy person. I will fix it."

And then I feel the electric razor running over my scalp, much closer to the surface than I would like. But I suppose she's right. It needs to be evened out.

A few minutes later, the razor shuts off. Helga takes a step back, admiring the finished product. "I am finished."

I reach into my purse to take out my phone, eager to see how this looks. I've been growing out my hair for ten years, and it's very nice to have a change. I should have done this years ago! I bring up the camera app on my phone, turn it around so that I can look at my reflection, and…

Oh my God.

I look *terrible.*

I hadn't quite realized how short she buzzed my hair. I had imagined a stylish pixie cut, but this is not that. The strands of my hair are universally about a centimeter long, and the lack of hair framing my face makes me look almost gaunt. And the short yellow hairs on the top of my head resemble the peach fuzz of a baby chick.

Then again, I'm not sure what kind of amazing haircut I was expecting from a half-blind lady in the back of a pawn shop.

Still, it's much worse than I even imagined. My eyes fill with tears as I stare at my reflection. What did I do to myself? What a horrible mistake. And for what? A stupid Christmas present?

"Do not be sad," Helga says in that sage-like way of hers. "This is love. You sacrifice for him. He sacrifices for you."

She's right. If Justin and I are married for the next fifty years, we will always remember the sacrifice I made for him. My hair will grow back.

"Thank you," I say.

She nods. "Merry Christmas, Stella."

CHAPTER 5

I never realized the extent to which my hair kept me warm until I have to walk home with my shorn head. Even though I have a hat on, the wind goes right through it. My scalp is freezing.

First order of business: obtain a warmer hat.

The snow is coming down harder now, so I pick up my pace. Helga put the watch chain in a small box, and she even put a layer of gift wrapping on it. I am so ready to exchange gifts with Justin. He may have gotten me something great, but I bet this present will bring tears to his eyes. That watch means so much to him.

I recognize our building from down the block because it's the one with the short awning that is torn to shreds like a starving moth had a go at it. This was the cheapest apartment we could find, and we can barely afford it. Both of us have loans—mine from college, and Justin's from college and law school—and every day it just feels like we are falling deeper into the hole. I work my two jobs, and

Justin had a job last year, but he gave it up this year because it was affecting his grades too much. That's why I picked up extra shifts at the diner.

I duck into the building, making sure to close the door behind me because the crime is terrible in this neighborhood. My beanie is damp from the snow, but I leave it on. When Justin sees my hair, he will demand an explanation, and I don't want to ruin the surprise.

We live on the fourth floor, and there's no elevator, so I climb the multiple flights of stairs to get to our apartment, my blister families throbbing the whole time. I don't know what Justin and I will do on Christmas day, but I can tell you it *won't* involve a lot of walking.

When I get to apartment 4-E, my key sticks in the lock the way it always does. When I finally get it to turn, Justin is sitting in the living room, the television blasting at full volume. I fight off a surge of annoyance that he has been sitting here watching Netflix all day while I worked a double shift. He could have gotten a job, at least for the holidays. The stores are always looking for men to play Santa Claus.

But before I have a chance to get too angry, Justin shuts off the television and comes to greet me at the door. He's wearing socks and a pair of sweatpants, his light brown hair adorably ruffled—it's hard to stay mad at him. The first thing he does is plant a kiss on my lips.

"Merry Christmas, Mrs. Hansen," he says to me. I love

it when he calls me that.

I laugh. "Is it after midnight already?"

Justin runs a hand through his short hair to smooth it out. I'm jealous that his hair is now longer than mine. "Barely. I was getting worried about you. I thought you left at eleven."

I smile secretly. "I had to make a pit stop."

"Oh yeah?" He steps back to let me come into the apartment. I can't help but notice a burning smell wafting from the kitchen. "That sounds interesting."

I shake off my winter coat and Justin tries to take it from me to hang up, but I wave him away. He never hangs stuff up properly—he just throws them on the hanger, sliding half off. So I pull open the closet and grab a hanger for my coat, although I leave my hat on. Just as I'm closing the door, I notice Justin moved our large suitcase to the hall closet.

Hmm. I wonder if his gift to me is some sort of vacation together. I could certainly go for that.

As I'm following him into the living room, I take a quick peek at our tiny kitchen, and when I see what's inside, I let out a cry of dismay. I don't know what Justin was doing, but our kitchen is a *disaster*. It looks like something exploded. There are pots and pans everywhere, and there's something brown smeared all over the counter that I hope to God is chocolate.

I've been working for twelve hours straight while he's been home all day. And somehow I return home to this mess? Who is supposed to clean up that kitchen? It better not be me.

Okay, I can't let myself get upset over this. This is our first Christmas together as husband and wife, and I'm about to give him the present of a lifetime. I'll worry about the messy kitchen later.

"Hey," Justin says as he reaches for my hat, "let me get that for you."

"No." I jerk away before he can get his hands on it. "I'm… cold."

"Really? The heat is back on. Should I turn it up?"

I shake my head. "Don't worry—I'll warm up soon. Let's exchange presents first."

Justin's face lights up. Despite our agreement not to spend too much on presents, he is clearly excited about this gift exchange. I absolutely did the right thing. In so many ways, my husband is like a little boy. He even has that boyish handsomeness. And you can't disappoint somebody like that on Christmas.

We head over to the sofa, so I can get off my feet. The sofa is right in front of our Christmas tree, which is admittedly not too impressive. We couldn't afford a really great tree, and even if we could, we don't have room for it in this tiny apartment. But we have a tree, and it's beautifully decorated with tinsel and ornaments. It sets the perfect mood for me to hand my gift-wrapped present to my husband. He grins at me and shakes the box.

"Wow," he says. "What is this?"

"You'll never guess."

He shakes it again, next to his ear. "Is it... a new puppy?"

I laugh. "Open it!"

He tears through the wrapping paper, depositing the shreds on our coffee table. I am nearly levitating with excitement when he takes the lid off the box. He peers inside, his lips pursed.

"You bought me..." He cocks his head to the side. "A necklace?"

"It's a chain for your pocket watch!"

"Oh!" He pulls it out, examining the silver links. "Wow, that's amazing, Stella. Thank you."

He looks happy. Although honestly, I thought he'd be a *little* happier. I thought he would be over the moon, but instead, he's just smiling politely. But I'm sure once he attaches it to the pocket watch, he'll recognize what an amazing present it is.

"This, um..." He bites his lip. "It looks expensive. I thought we weren't spending a lot on presents this year?"

"I got it for free, actually," I say proudly.

He raises an eyebrow. "You did?"

"Yes." And with that confession, I finally pull off my hat, revealing my buzzed hair. "I sold my hair to pay for it."

"You *what*?"

Justin couldn't have looked more astonished if I told him I sold a kidney to buy the watch chain. His jaw looks like it's about to unhinge.

"I found this pawn shop," I explain. "I tried to pawn a necklace, but it wasn't worth anything. But then they said that they would take my hair so I could get you that watch chain."

"Wait, let me get this straight." Justin rubs his temples with the tips of his fingers. "You sold your *hair* to buy me a necklace for my watch?"

"It's a *watch chain*," I say through my teeth. "I thought you'd be *happy*."

Justin sinks back against the sofa, a glazed expression on his face. This is hardly the reaction I expected. I had imagined he would be tenderly kissing me right now and we would end up making love right here on the sofa. Instead, he looks like he's completely disgusted with me.

"Well," I say finally, "what did you get for me?"

He stares at me for another moment before heaving himself to his feet. "It's in the kitchen. I'll go get it."

I squeeze my hands together, excitedly anticipating my gift. I can't imagine it could be better than the watch chain, but my husband is a very thoughtful man. So I am pretty excited right now.

Justin returns to the living room. He's holding a pan, which contains what looks like brownies. There's a red bow on top.

"Merry Christmas," he says.

I frown. "What's that?"

"Brownies," he says. "I made them for you. From scratch."

I look around, certain that I'm going to see some other present hidden away somewhere. There's no way my only present for our first Christmas as husband and wife could possibly be a tray of brownies. *Burnt* brownies, from the looks of it.

"Let me get a knife to cut them," he says.

He hurries back to the kitchen. Okay, this is going to be the switch. He's leading me to believe that my only present is these incinerated brownies, and now he's going to bring out the *real* present.

"Hey, Stella!" he calls out. "Where are all the knives?"

"In the drawer under the microwave!" I call back.

"Are you sure? All I see in there is like ten thousand spoons."

I hear a crash as something hits the floor. Men are so helpless—I'm itching to get up and help him, but I don't want to spoil the surprise. Finally, he yells out, "Found it!" I smile to myself, waiting to see the incredible present he's got for me.

Except when he comes out of the kitchen, all he's got in his hand is a knife.

I watch silently as he cuts me a square from the brownie tray. "I know you like the end piece," he says.

The brownies are rock-hard, so it takes some serious effort on his part to free one of them from the pan. When he gets it loose, about five billion crumbs scatter all over the coffee table, rug, and sofa.

"I'll clean that up," he says. Yeah, right.

I accept the brownie from my husband. The surface has zero give. This brownie has been baked within an inch of its life—no wonder the entire house smells like burning chocolate. I attempt to take a bite, but I'm not sure it's humanly possible. At least not without breaking a few teeth.

"I can't eat this," I say.

"I know it's a little overcooked…"

"It's incinerated."

The corner of his lips quirks up. "Well, I tried. That's what matters, isn't it?"

"Are you serious?"

"Serious about what?"

I fold my arms across my chest. "Are you seriously telling me that your only present to me this Christmas is a tray of burned brownies?"

"Hey!" He raises his hands. "We promised we weren't

going to buy expensive presents. I did the best I could on our budget."

"You did the best you could?" I cry. "I *sold my hair!*"

Justin's face turns pink. "Well, who asked you to do that? I didn't want you to do it!"

"I did it for you!" I cry. "Because I love you, and I wanted to get you an amazing present!"

"An amazing present? I barely even know what that thing is. What the hell am I supposed to do with it?"

"It's a watch chain! You chain your watch to things with it!"

"Why the hell would I want to do *that*?"

"The point is," I say, "I sacrificed something *important* to me to get you a great present!"

"You know what would have been an even *better* present?" he shoots back. "My wife not shaving herself *bald* to get me a watch necklace."

"I'm not bald!"

"Well, you don't have hair! I'd call that bald."

My face burns. I don't know if we have ever had a fight this big, and I can't believe we're having it during our first Christmas together as man and wife. Yet, I am *furious* with him. I don't know if I've *ever* been this angry before.

"*All* I have done is sacrifice for you," I snap at him. "I work two jobs so that you can focus on your studies. I took the late shift on Christmas Eve. I even *sold my hair* to get you an amazing present. And what do I get? Burnt brownies."

With those words, I pick up the tray of brownies and throw them across the room. They land at the base of our tree, which isn't substantial enough to withstand the blow of those rock-hard brownies. The tree teeters for a second or two before toppling over, spilling ornaments all over the floor. The sound of glass shattering fills the room.

"Jesus Christ," Justin breathes.

"What? It's not like you're the one who decorated the tree. That was all me—as usual."

"You're acting like a crazy person, you know that?" Justin shakes his head. "My God, you're worse than your mother."

Worse than *my mother*? Oh my God, he did *not* just accuse me of that.

"I mean, what's *wrong* with you?" he goes on. "Why would you possibly think I'd want you to shave your head like that?"

"I did it because I love you," I say in a small voice.

"Seriously, I know we don't have any money, but you need to go see that therapist." He pounds a fist on his knee to emphasize his point. "I mean it. I can't tolerate this kind of crazy behavior anymore."

Justin continues talking, ticking off on his fingers all my many flaws and how he's not even sure he can live with me anymore and we need some *time apart*. It sounds like he's been planning this.

Wait, is *that* why our suitcase is in the closet? Has he been planning to *leave*?

I don't know why he's doing this to me. I got him an amazing gift, and after all that, he didn't even *like* the gift. I thought this watch chain would fix our problems, but it feels like it's made everything worse.

Oh God, he is *still* going on and on. Why won't he stop? I wish he would just shut up.

And all the time he's talking, I keep looking at the knife he used to cut the brownies. He left it on the coffee table, and it's just sitting there. And I can't help but think that I bet a knife would make him stop talking.

Maybe for good.

CHAPTER 6

I never thought I would come back to Helga's Attic, and yet only a day after trading my hair for that watch chain, here I am.

I wasn't sure if the store would be open on Christmas day, but Helga said she's always open. Sure enough, when I get to the store, the lights are on inside. And when I open the door, Helga is standing behind the counter, just like she was when I left yesterday. It's like she hasn't moved an inch.

"Merry Christmas, Stella," she says to me.

"Merry Christmas, Helga," I say.

Like yesterday, my eyes are drawn to that large skull she keeps on the shelf by the entrance. Not that I would know, but it looks very realistic. And given that the woman collects human hair, why not a human skull? I'm dying to know, but of course, it's none of my business.

"How may I help you today?" Helga asks.

"Well…" I tug the sky-blue cap off my skull. "I was actually hoping to purchase a wig. It turns out short hair is not a good look on me."

"Yes," Helga says thoughtfully. "You may be right. However, you should know that my wigs are very expensive."

"I was hoping we could make a trade."

She hesitates for only a moment. "Very well."

She leads me to the corner of the store. There are half a dozen wigs atop the disembodied heads of mannequins. My own hair is not on display yet, which I suppose makes sense. It must take time to create a wig.

"Also, you should know," Helga adds, "that all of our wigs come with a set of ornamental combs."

She digs around in a chest by the wigs until she pulls out a small box. I open it up, and inside is the most beautiful set of tortoiseshell combs. It is the loveliest Christmas gift I could imagine.

Helga squints up at me with her cloudy pupils. "Do you want to be blond again?"

"No," I say thoughtfully. I run my hand through one of the red wigs. I wonder what I'd look like wearing it. People probably wouldn't even recognize me. "I think it's time for a change, don't you?"

She clears her throat. "What do you wish to trade for one of my wigs?"

I reach into my pocket. I pull out a pocket watch with a silver chain attached to it and hold it out to her.

"This is a lovely piece." She clutches the chain of the watch with her gnarled hands. She runs her thumb over the glass cover, halting on a dark red stain. Her eyes widen in alarm.

"That's, um, tomato sauce," I quickly explain. "It will wash right off."

"Yes," she says. "I am sure."

I hold my breath as she considers the trade. Finally, she lifts her eyes. "Yes. This is acceptable."

She returns to her desk and places the watch in a drawer. But the whole time, she doesn't take her eyes off me. I'm not sure if she believes the stain on that watch is tomato sauce. I should probably take my wig and be on my way.

After all, it's Christmas Day. There's quite a lot to do.

EPILOGUE

Helga

Stella leaves my store with her new wig and the set of combs I gave her. She is smiling and singing to herself, which is very different from the way she left last night.

Hair is power. In my many years of making wigs, I have been reminded of this fact again and again. When I took Stella's hair last night, I took her power. But now she has taken it back.

This was not how I wanted it to go. Not at all.

The sound of the rotary phone ringing echoes through my store. My daughter Angela is always begging me to buy one of those cellular phones, but I do not trust those strange things. I will use a rotary phone until the day I die.

When I pick up the receiver, Angela's sweet voice is on the other line. She is the light of my life—my reason for waking up every morning. And now that my Sven is gone, she is the only one who calls me.

"Merry Christmas, Mom!" she chirps. She sounds the happiest I have heard her in many weeks.

It won't last.

"Merry Christmas, my Angela," I choke out.

"I can't believe you're open on Christmas," she laughs. Her laughter has always reminded me of bells ringing. My precious daughter is everything to me, and so is her happiness.

"Well," I say, "there was business to be done."

"You work too hard, Mom."

I have to work hard. After Sven died of a heart attack, I had to support myself and Angela all on my own. But Angela turned out very well. She is the first in our family to go to college, and after that, she went to law school. She is in her second year now. I am so proud.

But it has not been smooth sailing. Last year, my Angela met a man. She fell instantly in love with this man, who turned out to be married. *You don't know what it's like to meet the man of your dreams, then meet his beautiful wife,* she sobbed to me.

I told Angela this was silliness. She is a beautiful girl. She can find a man who is not married and cheating on his wife. She said she has fallen in love, but I tell her to fall *out* of love.

But then a few weeks ago, she told me something different. She told me she has the child of this married man growing inside her.

After that, it was no longer silliness. This man who was the father of my grandchild would have to marry my daughter. And I would have to make it happen because I would do anything for Angela.

That is how I decided to find Stella.

It was very easy. I camped out outside their apartment building and followed her to the diner where she works. I realized she is not so beautiful after all. It was all her hair. Her beautiful hair—the source of her power over her husband.

I waited for the right moment. Angela told me all about Justin's precious pocket watch. I am very good at manipulating people. And Stella was remarkably easy to manipulate.

Hair is power. In the Bible, the source of Samson's strength was his hair, and when the beautiful Delilah tricked him and cut it off, she stripped him of his power. Similarly, I was certain that if I could take Stella's hair, I could take her power.

My hands are riddled with arthritis, and I haven't made a wig in years, but I would make one last wig. Out of Stella's hair, so I could give it to my daughter to ensure that her child—my first grandchild—would have a father.

But as I run my finger over the smear of red on the pocket watch, I fear it is too late.

"So, Mom," Angela says, "I have some amazing news."

I perk up. "Yes?"

"Yes." She takes a deep breath. "I called Justin yesterday and told him all about the baby. He told me he wants to raise the baby with me, and after the holidays, he's going to tell his wife that it's all over."

"He… he is?"

"Yes! He says he doesn't want to spoil their Christmas, so he's going to tell her tomorrow. He's already got a bag packed, and he's going to move out." I can hear her smiling, even through the phone. "I was trying to call you to tell you yesterday, but you weren't answering. This is why you need to get a cell phone, Mom!"

I drop the pocket watch on the desk. Some of the red material has rubbed off on my fingers.

"This is all I ever wanted," Angela sighs. "Sometimes Christmas wishes really do come true."

My daughter seems so happy. I cannot tell her the truth.

After we hang up, I walk over to the shelf near the entrance. I gently stroke the skull that I keep there at all times, tracing the cheekbones with my fingertip. Even though it is with the other items for sale, there is no price tag on the skull. It is not for sale.

"What have I done, Sven?" I wail. "I only wanted to help our daughter."

But of course, he has no answer for me. He never does—not anymore.

Angela will eventually discover the truth, but not today. Today, she will enjoy the holiday and continue to make plans for her unborn child. As for me, I walk over to the door of Helga's Attic and turn the lock. I will close the store for the rest of the day. It is, after all, Christmas Day.

THE END

ACKNOWLEDGMENTS

As this is a novelette (whatever that is, right?), I'll keep this short and sweet.

Thank you to everyone who read through this and gave me advice, including my mother, Pam, Kate, and Emily. Thank you to Avery for your cover expertise. And a special thanks to my husband, who helped me out with the ending. Believe it or not, he has some good advice that doesn't involve cows or conjoined twins.

Made in the USA
Coppell, TX
26 July 2023

19608264R00030